The Adventures of Sinbad

©2006 Alligator Books Limited

Published by Alligator Books Limited
Gadd House, Arcadia Avenue
London N3 2JU

Printed in Malaysia

Many years ago in an ancient eastern city there lived a young man whose name was Sinbad. His father, who was very rich, died and left his son a great deal of money. But in a short while Sinbad had foolishly wasted most of his father's wealth.

With what little money he had left, Sinbad decided to buy goods to trade in other lands. So he boarded a ship with several other merchants and put to sea.

"Our fortunes will be made on this voyage!" Sinbad called cheerfully to the men as the ship sailed out of the harbour.

Time went by and Sinbad's ship journeyed far across the ocean. Wherever it stopped, at ports or islands, people were eager to buy the merchant's goods in return for gold and silver, and Sinbad became a rich man once more.

One day, as the ship was passing a small island, the captain suggested that everyone might like to go ashore. Sinbad and the others had only been there for a short while when the whole island started to shudder and shake.

Suddenly, out of the water, rose the gigantic head of a sea monster! Fortunately the terrified men were thrown off its back before the monster dived beneath the waves.

The moment the captain thought everybody had returned safely to the ship he set sail, but in the confusion Sinbad was left behind clinging to a piece of wood.

And before that day was out, the swift current had taken him to the shores of another island.

Soon enough, Sinbad was discovered and taken before the King who ruled the island. The King was so impressed that Sinbad had managed to stay alive, he gave him a chest full of gold and a fast ship to carry him home.

Although Sinbad returned to his city a very rich man, he soon grew bored and longed for further adventures. Then one day a group of merchants asked Sinbad to join them on their next voyage.

All went well until they landed on a faraway desert island, where, by some strange chance Sinbad was left behind once more. And when he gazed out to sea from the top of a palm tree, the ship was almost out of sight.

It was then he noticed a giant white ball near the beach, so he climbed down to investigate. Suddenly out of the sky a gigantic bird flew towards him. (He had often heard sailors tell of a fearsome bird called a Roc.)

As soon as the Roc sat down on its huge egg, Sinbad tied himself to the bird's leg with his turban, and when the Roc took off, Sinbad was carried away from the desert island.

The Roc flew high over the sea, and on reaching the mountains, it swooped down into a deep valley.

When the giant bird landed, Sinbad just managed to untie the knot of his turban before the Roc seized a serpent in its beak and flew away.

Sinbad looked about him and saw that the ground was covered in enormous diamonds, but coiled between the gems lay massive serpents dozing in the sun.

As he stood holding his sword in case the serpents awoke, something fell from the cliffs high above. When Sinbad glimpsed men standing on top of the cliffs, he quickly worked out what was happening.

They were hurling large pieces of meat onto the diamonds below, for they knew that the mountain eagles would fly down. The gems would stick to the meat, and then be carried back to the eagles' nests, where the men could collect them.

Now Sinbad knew of a way to escape! He picked up the biggest diamond and stuck it onto a piece of meat, and when the next eagle swooped down, he grabbed its legs and was carried out of the valley to safety.

And so it was, when Sinbad returned home, he was able to sell the magnificent diamond he had brought from the Valley of the Serpents and give the money to the poor in his city.

Sinbad had only been back for a while when he began to find life rather dull, so he chartered a ship and set sail once more.

After travelling for many days, the ship ran into a terrible storm. Very soon strong winds and towering waves drove it close to an island.

Before Sinbad and the other sailors could swim to the shore, hordes of savage creatures clambered up the sides of the ship and swarmed all over the deck.

Sinbad and the rest of the men were overpowered and dragged off to a castle on the island.

They were taken before a hideous giant with one bulging eye that stared out of the middle of his forehead.

"Perhaps they will hold us for ransom or make us work as slaves," whispered Sinbad.

That night they were locked up in prison, and next morning were sent to work in the giant's forest. Seeing so many logs lying on the ground gave Sinbad an idea!

In the days that followed, whenever the guards turned their backs, the sailors built rafts that they managed to hide.

Late one night, when the guards had fallen asleep, Sinbad and his friends made their escape from the castle. They hurried down to the shore where the rafts were hidden, jumped aboard and rowed quickly away from that awful island.

Most of the rafts were large and could carry several men. One raft was smaller than the rest, but it was big enough for Sinbad.

As the men pulled on their oars and sped swiftly into the darkness, Sinbad's raft was caught in a whirlpool!

The raft spun round and round then vanished, and poor Sinbad was tossed into the raging sea. Luckily by morning he had been washed up on a beach.

As he came to his senses Sinbad heard a hissing sound. Slithering across the beach was a huge serpent!

In fear for his life, Sinbad climbed to the top of the nearest tree with the serpent close behind.

By great good fortune, some sailors on a passing ship heard Sinbad's desperate cries. They sent a boat to pick him up and frightened off the serpent with a hail of arrows.

11

With Sinbad safely aboard, his rescuers listened in awe to his incredible story. Then, without any warning, a powerful wave dashed the ship against a jagged rock. Sinbad and the crew had scarcely time to jump off before the ship sank near an island.

The water was shallow, and when the men waded ashore, they discovered hundreds of chests overflowing with treasure – so many ships had been wrecked in that place and their valuable cargo washed up on the beach.

With all that treasure spread before them, the men could go home rich beyond their wildest dreams.

But unfortunately they had been shipwrecked at the foot of a high mountain with sides too steep to climb!

Sinbad was puzzled. A vast river of dark water flowed *from* the sea and disappeared through a cavern into the mountain.

"Could this be a means to escape?" wondered Sinbad.

When he explained to the men
what he planned to do, without a
moment's hesitation, they gathered
up the ship's timber that littered
the shore and built a strong raft,
and on top they loaded a cargo of
gold and precious stones.

"When I reach safety, I promise
to send a ship for you and the rest
of the treasure!" called Sinbad as
he leapt aboard.

Swiftly the river took him
through the mouth of the
cavern and deep into
the mountain.

The water swept the raft along.
Very soon Sinbad found himself in
total darkness and after many hours
he fell into a deep sleep.

When he awoke it was daylight.
A group of people on the bank
were surprised to see a stranger
floating by. They tied his raft to a
tree, and brought a fine horse for
Sinbad to ride to the city of Serendib
to meet the King.

The first thing the King did when
he had listened to Sinbad's story was
to send a ship to rescue the sailors
still left behind.

During the days that followed,
Sinbad and the King became great
friends. And when Sinbad left for his
own city, the King entrusted him with
a letter of friendship and costly gifts
for his ruler,
the Caliph,
so great was
his faith
in Sinbad.

After a long journey Sinbad reached home. Straight away he delivered the letter and gifts to the Caliph, who was delighted.

"You must go back to the King of Serendib with gifts from me in return for his friendship."

So Sinbad was forced to set sail once more, as the Caliph could not be disobeyed. When he arrived in Serendib, the King was overjoyed to see Sinbad again, and was greatly honoured by the Caliph's gifts.

But alas, on the way home, Sinbad's ship was attacked by pirates!

They took the ship and all the treasure that had been loaded on board from the King of Serendib.

The pirates captured Sinbad and the crew and chained them up in the hold. Worse still, they were sold as slaves in the next port.

Sinbad was bought by a wealthy merchant and taken to join the rest of his many servants. Although he was now a slave, his life was not hard.

The merchant had a beautiful daughter named Yasmin, and as the time passed Sinbad fell in love with her.

One early morning the merchant sent for Sinbad. "Slave! I have a special task for you. In the forest lives the biggest of all elephants. Tonight, when the moon shines full, he will come to drink at the pool nearby. Take this bow and arrow and shoot him, or I will have you killed!"

Sinbad was horrified for he knew the merchant wanted the elephant's valuable ivory tusks to sell. What was he to do?

That night Sinbad set off towards the forest as the merchant had ordered.

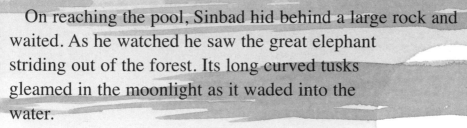

On reaching the pool, Sinbad hid behind a large rock and waited. As he watched he saw the great elephant striding out of the forest. Its long curved tusks gleamed in the moonlight as it waded into the water.

Sinbad stepped forward cautiously, then he saw to his astonishment, the merchant's beautiful daughter sitting on the elephant. At first when Yasmin noticed Sinbad she was very upset.

"My father is a cruel man. That is why I come here at night to protect this gentle creature," she cried. "Shoot me instead! For I would rather die myself than let this beautiful elephant die!"

"Tonight I came to the pool to *save* the elephant," explained Sinbad. "I know your father is waiting for me to bring back its ivory tusks, but I planned to ride away on the elephant to freedom."

Yasmin had never felt happier in her life when she heard what Sinbad said, for now her beloved elephant would be saved from the cruellest of fates.

"I have no wish to return to my father," sighed Yasmin, "but where shall I go?"

"Come and live in my city," said Sinbad. Yasmin gladly agreed (for secretly she had fallen in love with him the moment he was brought to the house as a slave).

The two journeyed through many different lands, they travelled across hot deserts, wide plains and high mountains, but Yasmin and Sinbad were safe every step of the way on the back of their elephant.

When they came in sight of Sinbad's city, the Caliph's own barge was waiting to carry them across the water.

Great were the celebrations when people saw the golden barge arrive, for Sinbad had come home at last.

When tales of his incredible adventures were told, Sinbad became famous throughout the land.

He never put to sea again and gave most of the riches he had made from his voyages to the poor…and Yasmin and Sinbad lived happily ever after.